What do you feel like when you dance?

feel I'm getting my grooves.
— Frankie

A little shy, but happy too.
— Mae

When I jump, I feel
like I'm flying.
— Sammy

I feel a little dizzy
when I spin around.
— Charlie

Happy and calm.
— Harriet

I feel excited and fizzy inside.
— Riley

Sink your fangs into an Isadora Moon adventure!

Isadora Moon Goes to School

Isadora Moon Goes Camping

Isadora Moon Goes to the Ballet

Coming soon!

Isadora Moon Has a Birthday

ISADORA MOON

Goes to the Ballet

Harriet Muncaster

A STEPPING STONE BOOK™

Random House 🏠 New York

For vampires, fairies, and humans everywhere!
And for Nicola, who loves the ballet.

Copyright © 2016 by Harriet Muncaster
Cover art copyright © 2016 by Harriet Muncaster

All rights reserved. Published in the United States by
Random House Children's Books, a division of Penguin Random House LLC,
New York. Originally published in paperback by
Oxford University Press, Oxford, in 2016.

Random House and the colophon are registered trademarks and
A Stepping Stone Book and the colophon are trademarks of
Penguin Random House LLC.

Visit us on the Web!
SteppingStonesBooks.com
rhcbooks.com

Educators and librarians, for a variety of teaching tools,
visit us at RHTeachersLibrarians.com

Library of Congress Cataloging-in-Publication Data is available upon request.
ISBN 978-0-399-55829-0 (hc) — ISBN 978-0-399-55830-6 (lib. bdg.) —
ISBN 978-0-399-55831-3 (pbk.) — ISBN 978-0-399-55832-0 (ebook)

MANUFACTURED IN CHINA
10 9 8 7 6 5 4 3 2 1
First American Edition

This book has been officially leveled by using the
F&P Text Level Gradient™ Leveling System.

Random House Children's Books supports the
First Amendment and celebrates the right to read.

ISADORA MOON

Goes to the Ballet

Chapter One

Isadora Moon, that's me! And this is Pink Rabbit. He is my best friend. We do everything together. Some of our favorite things include flying near the stars in the night sky, having glitter tea parties with my

bat-patterned tea set, and practicing our ballet.

We have been practicing our ballet a lot recently and putting on shows for Mom and Dad. I have discovered that Dad's vampire cape makes a great stage curtain! It looks especially nice with silver-star sequins glued onto it . . . though I am not sure Dad agrees. He seemed a little . . . annoyed last time he saw his best cape being used as a stage curtain.

"It's covered in stars!" he complained. "I'm not a wizard—I'm a vampire! Vampires don't have starry capes."

I felt bad then, but it was okay because Mom waved her wand, and the stars all disappeared. She can do things like that because she's a fairy. She was the one who brought Pink Rabbit to life for me.

"Good as new!" she said, sitting down on one of the chairs Pink Rabbit and I had put out for the audience. Dad sat down too, with my baby sister, Honeyblossom, on his lap, and they all waited for our show to begin.

"Right," I whispered to Pink Rabbit once

we were behind the non-starry curtain. "Can you remember your moves?"

Pink Rabbit nodded and did a perfect leap. He's been getting very good at ballet lately. I gave him a thumbs-up.

"Let's go!" I whispered.

Together we leapt out from behind the curtain in a magnificent jump. Mom and Dad clapped and cheered. Pink Rabbit began to twirl on his tippy-toes. I swirled and twirled in my glittering black tutu.

"Excellent!" called Dad.

"Enchanting!" said Mom, waving her wand so that we were showered with pink flower petals.

At the end of the show, I gave a deep curtsy
and Pink Rabbit bowed, and Mom and Dad

cheered some more. Even Honeyblossom clapped her chubby little hands.

"That was really wonderful!" said Mom. "And so professional!"

Pink Rabbit looked proud and puffed out his chest in his striped waistcoat.

"One day you'll both be prima ballerinas!" said Dad.

"I hope so!" I said as we both tiptoed gracefully across the floor. We followed Mom and Dad down the stairs and into the kitchen for breakfast. It was seven o'clock at night, but we always have two breakfasts in our house. One in the morning and one in the evening. That is because Dad sleeps during the day. He has his breakfast in the evening, before going out for his nightly fly.

"I want to be just like Tatiana Tutu!" I said as I began to spread peanut butter on a piece of toast. Tatiana Tutu is my favorite ballerina of all time.

I have never seen her in real life, but I always watch when she's on TV, and I have a special scrapbook filled with pictures of

7

her. I cut the pictures out of magazines and decorate them with starry sequins and silver glitter.

I also have a big poster of Tatiana Tutu on my bedroom wall. She is wearing a sparkling black tutu and her famous star diamond tiara. Her black tutu looks exactly

like the kind a vampire-fairy might wear. . . .
It looks just like mine!

"If you keep practicing and work hard
at your ballet, I'm sure you'll be as good as
Tatiana Tutu one day," said Dad as he poured
himself a glass of his red juice. Dad only ever
drinks red juice. It's a vampire thing.

"Yes," said Mom. "Keep practicing and one day maybe we'll come to watch you and Pink Rabbit perform in a real theater!"

Pink Rabbit bounced up and down.

Chapter Two

The next day at school, I told my friends all about the ballet show Pink Rabbit and I put on for Mom and Dad.

"That sounds like so much fun!" said Zoe. "Can I come to your house and we can do it again? I could wear my pink tutu and be the Sugar Plum Fairy!"

11

"And I could wear my white tutu and be a dancing snowflake," said Samantha dreamily.

"I'll be the hero of the show," said Oliver, jumping in. "I'll wear a mask and my black cape!"

"There could be an intermission with refreshments," suggested Bruno. "We could hand out cookies to the audience."

"Or candy," said Sashi. "That's what you're supposed to have at intermission."

"I love candy!" yelled Zoe.

Just then Miss Cherry came into the room. Miss Cherry is our teacher at human school, and she is very nice. She doesn't mind that I am a vampire-fairy. She treats me just the same as everyone else.

"Good morning," she said, smiling. "I have some exciting news for you all today." She started to hand out some letters, giving one to each person.

"We are going on a school trip," she said. "To see a ballet!"

"A ballet!" said Zoe. "We were just talking about putting on a pretend ballet!"

"Well, here's your chance to see a real one," said Miss Cherry. "We are going to see the *Alice in Wonderland* ballet!"

I felt my heart beat faster. A ballet! We were going to see a real ballet!

"You need to take the letter home and get your parents to sign it," said Miss Cherry. "We also need some parents to volunteer to help on the trip."

"Will there be cookies at intermission?" called out Bruno.

"I expect there will be candy," said Miss Cherry.

"I told you," whispered Sashi.

"There will be a famous ballerina playing the part of the White Rabbit," continued Miss Cherry. "You might have heard of her if you are interested in ballet. Her name is Tatiana Tutu."

"TATIANA TUTU!" I shouted, jumping up from my chair. The whole class turned to look at me.

"Yes," said Miss Cherry. "You obviously know who she is, Isadora."

Tatiana Tutu

"I do," I said in a smaller voice, suddenly embarrassed. I sat down quickly, feeling my face go pink.

Pink Rabbit didn't seem embarrassed at all. He did a little hop and wiggled his ears. He was beside himself with excitement that Tatiana Tutu was going to play the part of the *rabbit*.

As soon as I got home, I showed the letter to Mom.

"You have to sign it!" I said. "Quick! Or I can't go on the school trip."

"Hang on a second," said Mom. "Let me read it, Isadora. It says here that they need parents to volunteer for the trip."

"They do," I said, starting to feel worried. "But not you and Dad."

"Why not?" asked Mom. "We could volunteer! It would be good for us to get more involved with your school activities."

"It's in the daytime," I said. "Dad will be asleep."

"That's true," said Mom. "What a shame!"

I didn't think it was a shame at all. In fact, I felt relieved. But when Dad came down for breakfast that evening, he seemed very interested in the trip.

"I will volunteer!" he said enthusiastically. "I will make an exception! Hand me the pen!"

I held the pen behind my back.

"There's really no need for you both to come . . . ," I began.

But Mom swooped in with her wand and put a magic tick in the "volunteer" box.

"How exciting!" she said.

Chapter
Three

On the morning of the trip, I woke up early. But not as early as Pink Rabbit. When I opened my eyes, he was already up and bouncing around the bedroom, practicing his pliés and pirouettes.

"Today's the day we see Tatiana Tutu!" I said excitedly, hopping straight out of bed

and starting to get dressed. I put on my best outfit and then picked up Pink Rabbit's little waistcoat.

"You must wear this," I told him. "It's important to look fancy for the ballet."

Pink Rabbit let me put the waistcoat on him, and then we flew down the stairs to breakfast.

"Good morning," said Mom, who was already up and busy feeding Honeyblossom her bottle of pink milk. "I'm going to drop Honeyblossom off at the babysitter's in a minute," she said. "I'll meet you and Dad at the school. You can walk there with him."

"Okay," I said as I started to eat my breakfast.

I watched Mom fly around the kitchen, packing all the baby things in a bag. Then she went into the hall and put Honeyblossom into her stroller.

"See you soon, Isadora!" she called as they left the house.

I continued to sit at the table and eat my breakfast. It was very quiet without Mom and Honeyblossom.

"I hope Dad comes down soon," I said to

Pink Rabbit. He twitched his nose worriedly.

But Dad was nowhere to be seen. An awful thought struck me.

"I hope he hasn't overslept," I said. "It's almost time to leave!"

Together we jumped down from the table and flew up the stairs. I banged loudly on the door to Mom and Dad's bedroom. There was no answer. All I could hear was snoring.

"Oh dear," I whispered.

I pushed open the bedroom door. Dad was lying in bed with all the curtains closed and his eye mask on. He was fast asleep.

"Dad!" I shouted in a panic. "Wake up! We have to leave for the school trip!"

"Wha—" Dad jerked awake and sat bolt upright in bed. He ripped off his eye mask and looked frantically around the room.

"The school trip," I said. "It's today!"

"Oh no!" wailed Dad in dismay. "I've overslept."

"It's okay," I said. "If you can get ready in five minutes, we will still be on time."

"*Five minutes!*" said Dad. "I can't get ready in *five minutes*! It takes me half an hour just to do my hair!"

I sighed. Vampires are very picky about the way they look. They like to always be perfectly groomed.

"Well, we can't be late and hold everyone else up!" I told him.

Pink Rabbit and I went back down the stairs, and I put on my best cape. We waited by the door for five minutes.

"Dad!" I shouted. "It's time to go!"

He appeared at the top of the stairs. "All

right, all right, I'm coming," he grumbled. He didn't look like my dad at all. His hair was sticking up all over the place, and he was wearing a pair of mismatched socks.

"Honestly!" he complained as he made his way down the stairs. "What a time to have to be awake!"

I opened the front door, and the three of us stepped out into the frosty air. Together we walked along the garden path, through the gate, and down the road to school. We couldn't walk very fast because Dad kept stopping to look in car windows.

"I've just got to comb this section of hair," he explained. "And this part too."

Then an angry man rolled down his car window and shouted at Dad to stop staring at him. Dad jumped back in fright.

"I think I'll wait until we get to the school," he said, putting his comb away.

Chapter Four

When we arrived, Mom was there, wearing a bright pink safety vest. Miss Cherry was busy ticking names off a list.

"Wonderful!" she said, beaming at everyone. "We are all here!" She reached into her teacher's bag and pulled out another bright pink safety vest. She showed it to Dad.

"You need to wear this, Mr. Moon," she said. "It's so the children can see where you are at all times. It's for safety."

Dad looked horrified.

"I can't wear that," he protested. "It doesn't go with my outfit!"

"Don't be silly," said Mom. "Just put it on."

Dad put the vest on, but he didn't seem to be very happy about it.

"I look ridiculous," he sniffed. "Very un-vampirey."

Miss Cherry put her clipboard away and clapped her hands for silence.

"Is everyone ready?" she asked. "It's time to go!"

We all started to follow her toward the door, but I noticed that Dad was going in the opposite direction.

"I've got to finish doing my hair," he explained. "You all go on without me. I'll catch up! I won't be long!"

Dad rushed off to the bathroom while

the rest of us followed Miss Cherry out of the school and toward the train station in the middle of town. Everyone was excited and chatting loudly. I felt especially excited because I had never been on a train before.

"I can't believe you've never been on a train!" said Zoe, who was walking next to me and holding Pink Rabbit's other paw. "Everyone's been on a train before!"

"Not me," I told her. "My family mostly flies everywhere."

The train station was big and gray and noisy. The trains looked like giant metal caterpillars crawling up and down the tracks. Mom didn't seem too happy, and her fairy wings started to droop a little bit.

"Where are the flowers?" she asked. "Where are the forests? Where's all the lovely nature?"

She pointed her wand at a couple of empty gray hanging baskets that were fastened to the station wall. Bright pink flowers immediately sprouted out of them and cascaded over the sides.

"Much better," said Mom, smiling.

She waved her wand again, and this time grass started to shoot up all over the platform.

"Hey!" shouted a train conductor, starting to walk toward us and waving his ticket machine around. "What are you doing?"

"I'm just . . . ," began Mom, but her words were drowned out by the sound of a train pulling up next to us.

"Come on, everyone. Quickly!" said Miss Cherry, hurrying our group into the train car. She pressed the button to shut the door before the conductor could reach us.

Zoe pulled me toward a pair of seats, and we sat down as the train started to move away from the station.

I felt a fizz of excitement to be inside the huge clanking metal car. Pink Rabbit and I stared out the window. We watched as the houses and trees rushed past at lightning speed.

"It is almost like flying!" I said to Zoe.

As we chatted and looked at the scenery, Miss Cherry walked up and down the car, taking roll again.

"Just checking that everyone is on board," she said.

Everyone was. Except Dad.

Chapter
Five

"Oh dear," I said to Zoe. "I thought Dad would have caught up with us by now. I guess he won't be coming after all."

Just then Pink Rabbit began to wiggle around on my lap, pointing out the window with his paw. He had spotted something in the sky.

"What is it, Pink Rabbit?" I asked. "What do you see?"

We peered up into the sky and squinted.

"It's a bird," said Jasper. "A big black bird with a bright pink tummy."

"Hmm," I said, squinting harder. "I don't think it is a bird. . . . I think . . ."

"It's your dad!" squealed Zoe. "Your dad's flying toward us!"

We watched as Dad soared closer, his vampire cape flowing out behind him. Vampires can fly very fast, and it wasn't long before he was alongside the train, smiling in through the window.

"It's Isadora's dad!" screamed the class,

44

all standing up in the train car and pointing at him. "Look!"

Mom sighed in relief. "Thank sugarplum fairies for that!"

"Oh my goodness!" said Miss Cherry with her hands clasped. "That can't be safe!"

"Don't worry," said Mom, leaning over and patting Miss Cherry in a comforting way. "My husband is a very talented flier."

Dad continued to fly alongside the train until we stopped at the next station. Then

he stepped into the train and flopped down onto one of the seats.

"Phew!" he said. "That's my daily exercise completed!"

The class all cheered, and Miss Cherry gave a frazzled smile.

Chapter Six

When we got to the theater, I held on to Pink Rabbit's paw tightly. The entrance was very crowded. It made me feel all hot and prickly. So many people were jostling around, and it was very noisy. We had to wait in a line for a long time.

"Oh goodness!" said Mom, who is not

used to being in small, crowded spaces. She waved her wand so that a cool gust of air billowed around us.

Dad was busy looking at the posters of ballet dancers on the walls.

"Don't the men look nice?" he said, impressed. "They are almost as well dressed

as a vampire. That one even has a cape!"

"Everyone must stay together," called Miss Cherry, getting out her class list again.

"I want to buy candy," said Bruno, pointing at a stand.

"Me too!" said Oliver. "My mom gave me some money for food!"

Once Miss Cherry had taken roll again, we all scrambled toward the concession stand. Mom gave me money to buy chocolate stars, which are my favorite human treats. Zoe bought some sour candy with her money.

"I think I will have some strawberry laces," announced Dad. "They are the next-best thing to red juice."

Once we had all got our snacks, we

followed Miss Cherry up some stairs and through a dark little door.

"Welcome to the theater!" she said.

I felt my mouth drop open in amazement. We were in a *huge*, glittering auditorium. There were rows of velvet seats stretching all the way to the back and all the way up to the ceiling. At the front of the massive hall was a stage with a curtain across the front. Everything looked very fancy.

Miss Cherry led us toward a row of seats in the middle of the theater, and we all sat down.

"I can't wait to see the ballet dancers!" said Zoe.

"Me too," I said, popping a chocolate star into my mouth. "I especially can't wait to see Tatiana Tutu! Neither can Pink Rabbit." I reached out to lift him onto my lap so he could see the stage . . . but I didn't feel any squishy pink paws. . . .

Chapter Seven

I looked down.

Nothing.

My whole body went cold, and my skin started to prickle.

"Um," I said, putting the bag of chocolate stars down and suddenly feeling very sick. "Where's Pink Rabbit?"

Zoe frowned. "Isn't he here?" she asked. "You had him just before we bought our snacks."

"I was holding his paw!" I said in a panic. "I must have let go of him when I was choosing the chocolate stars! He probably got lost in the crowd!" I stood up from my chair.

"I have to go and find him," I said to Zoe. "Poor Pink Rabbit will be so scared."

I quickly made my way along the row

toward Mom and the door that led back to the entrance.

"Where are you going?" asked Miss Cherry as I approached. "Isadora, sit down, please. The show is going to start in a minute."

"I need to talk to my mom," I said, hurrying past her. "It's an emergency!"

"What is it?" asked Mom when I finally reached her.

"It's Pink Rabbit!" I said in a panicked voice. "He's gone!"

"Gone!" said Mom worriedly. "What do you mean?" She stood up and took my hand. Together we made our way out of the auditorium.

The entrance seemed very bright compared to the low light of the theater hall. It was quite empty now that most people had gone inside to find their seats. Mom and I looked all over for Pink Rabbit, but we didn't see him anywhere. He wasn't by the concession stand or by the bathrooms or

by the counter where you hand in your ticket. . . .

Where could he be?

We paced around and around the theater entrance, but he was nowhere to be seen.

"Pink Rabbit!" I called frantically. "Pink Rabbit, where are you?"

"Maybe he's outside," suggested Mom. "Let's have a look."

We made our way out the theater doors, but my eyes were all blurry with tears and I couldn't see where I was going.

"Sit down a minute," said Mom, giving me a hug. "Don't worry, Isadora. We'll find him. He couldn't have gone far." Together we sat down on the outdoor steps and breathed

in the cold winter air. Mom wiped my eyes with a pink fairy tissue that puffed sparkling dust all over my face.

"Oops," she said, "wrong tissue."

As we sat there, I noticed a small door a few feet down from the main theater entrance. Above it was a sign:

STAGE DOOR

I felt my hopes start to rise again.

"Mom, look!" I said, pointing. "Do you think that's where Pink Rabbit has gone?"

Mom looked doubtful.

"It's unlikely," she said. "That's the place where the actors and dancers go to get ready for the show. I don't see how Pink Rabbit could have got inside."

"Maybe he was pulled in with one of the dancers," I said hopefully. "I think we should check, just to be sure."

"Okay," said Mom.

Together we flew to the door and pushed it open. It wasn't locked, but there was a man sitting at a desk just inside.

"Hey!" he said. "You can't come in here. This entrance is for performers only."

"Oh dear," said Mom, getting flustered. "Well, it's just that . . . well, he's a pink rabbit, you see. . . . He's very special, and he's only very little. . . ."

As Mom made up a long story about

Pink Rabbit, I slipped quietly past the desk
and into the room behind.

Unlike the theater hall, where the
audience goes, this was not grand at all.
Ahead was a long gray hallway with lots
of doors on either side. Some of the doors

had names on them, but I didn't stop to look. I tiptoed silently past them all, past a rack of tutus and a box of used ballet shoes, down to the end of the hall, where I turned a corner . . .

And there was Pink Rabbit!

Chapter Eight

Pink Rabbit was standing alone in the middle of the hallway and looking very lost.

"Oh, Pink Rabbit!" I said, scooping him up into my arms and giving him an enormous hug. "I thought you had disappeared forever! What happened? Did you get confused and follow the wrong people?"

Pink Rabbit
nodded and
nuzzled into
my neck.

"Thank
goodness I
found you!" I said,
putting him down.
"We should get back to our seats now. We
don't want to miss the show!"

We started walking back down the hallway, Pink Rabbit holding my hand, when a
sudden sniffling noise made us stop. It was
coming from behind the nearest door, the
one with a big silver star, and it sounded
very sad.

"Oh dear," I whispered to Pink Rabbit. "What should we do?"

Pink Rabbit pointed toward the exit with his squishy pink paw, but I shook my head.

"We can't just leave," I whispered. "Not if

someone is upset. That's not a very kind thing to do. We should see if we can help."

Pink Rabbit bounced back in alarm.

"Come on," I said to him. "Let's be brave."

I lifted my hand and knocked on the door. The sniffling sound from inside stopped immediately. After a minute or so, the door opened and a beautiful lady peeked out. I could only see her eyes, but they were covered in silver glitter, and she had on a pair of false eyelashes.

"Hello?" she sniffed.

"Hello," I said in a small voice, suddenly feeling very shy. "We just wondered . . . if you . . . if you were all right?"

The lady gave a watery smile and blinked

her huge eyelashes. Then she opened the door wider so we could see more of her. She had a pair of white bunny ears on her head and was wearing a white leotard with a black velvet waistcoat. She was also balancing on one leg.

"The White Rabbit!" I gasped. "Tatiana Tutu! It's you!"

"It is," she said. "I am Tatiana Tutu. But who are you?"

"I'm Isadora Moon," I told her. "And this is Pink Rabbit."

Pink Rabbit put his paws behind his back and puffed out his chest importantly. Tatiana Tutu looked at him with interest for a moment, and then she opened the door all the way.

"Please, come in," she said.

Pink Rabbit and I slipped inside the room, and Tatiana Tutu closed the door behind us. I looked around and gasped in wonder.

The room was dazzling. There was a big mirror on the wall, with bright lightbulbs set around it, and from the ceiling hung rows of sparkling tutus. On Tatiana Tutu's dressing table was the famous star diamond tiara.

"Wow," I breathed, staring at it. "It's so pretty."

"You can try it on if you'd like," said Tatiana Tutu, picking the tiara up and putting it on my head. I gazed into the mirror and turned from side to side, watching the diamonds flash and twinkle in the light. My smile grew wider and wider.

"It looks good on you!" Tatiana Tutu said with a laugh. Then her face took on a more serious expression, and I remembered why we were here. I took the tiara off and laid it carefully on the dressing table.

"Why were you crying?" I asked her.

Tatiana Tutu sighed and looked sad.

"I hurt my leg," she explained, pointing at the one she was holding up in the air. "I tripped on the way to the theater. I thought it was going to be all right, but it's hurting very badly. I'm not sure I can dance on it tonight, and there's no time to get a replacement dancer now. The show will have to be canceled."

71

"What?" I gasped.

"Yes." Tatiana Tutu nodded, a tear trickling down her cheek. "And it's all my fault. I let everyone down."

"Oh no!" I said. "You can't help that you tripped. I trip over things all the time! Is there no other way the show can go on?"

"Not really," said Tatiana Tutu. "You can't have *Alice in Wonderland* without the White Rabbit, can you?"

"I suppose not," I said sadly.

"The other dancers are disappointed," continued Tatiana Tutu. "That's why it's so quiet backstage right now. Usually everyone's hustling and bustling around and looking forward to the show. But now it's like a ghost town!"

I nodded, and Tatiana Tutu looked at the clock on her dressing-room wall.

"The show should have started by now," she said. "The stage director will have to go out very soon and announce that it's canceled." She wiped a tear from her glittery eye and sniffed.

"Oh dear," I said. "I wish I could think of something that would help."

Pink Rabbit bounced up and down next to me and waved his paws in the air. Tatiana Tutu and I both turned to look at him. He did grand jetés across the room and then a perfect pirouette. He pointed his toes just like a real ballet dancer. Then he gave a deep bow.

"Oh," I said. "Wait a minute! I think I have an idea. . . ."

Chapter Nine

Zoe stared worriedly at me when Mom and I got back to our seats in the theater.

"You didn't find him?" she said. "Where's Pink Rabbit?"

"It's all right," I told her as I sat down in my chair. "I did find him but . . . he's busy."

"Busy?" said Zoe. "What do you mean?"

"It's a surprise!" I said. "You'll find out really soon!"

Zoe looked confused, but she didn't ask any more questions. "Okay . . . ," she said suspiciously.

We chatted quietly for a while longer. Then the lights in the theater went down and a great hush fell over the audience. The orchestra started to play, and the big velvet curtain began to rise. Zoe and I breathed out in wonderment. The stage didn't look like a stage but a beautiful garden. In the middle was a tree with frothy pink cherry blossoms all over it. The ballet dancer playing the part of Alice was sitting on one of the branches. She was wearing a white tutu with a black headband in her pale blond hair. Everything shone and sparkled, and the cherry blossom petals rained down from the tree. The music suddenly got faster, and the White Rabbit leapt on from stage left.

Except it wasn't a white rabbit. . . .

It was a little pink rabbit! My Pink Rabbit!

He looked very small up there on the stage, and I suddenly felt very nervous for him. But I also felt extremely proud.

Pink Rabbit tiptoed across the stage in his striped waistcoat. He was holding a pocket watch in his paw and looking at it as he leapt along.

"I'M LATE, I'M LATE, I'M LATE!" the music seemed to say.

Pink Rabbit bounced and bounded past the cherry blossom tree, and the dancer playing Alice jumped down and followed him. Together they danced around the pretend garden, twirling and soaring among the cherry blossom petals.

"Isadora," whispered Zoe. "Is that . . . is that—?"

"Pink Rabbit!" I whispered back. "Yes!"

"Wow!" breathed Zoe. "He's amazing!"

We watched as Pink Rabbit did a spin and then disappeared down a pretend

hole in the stage. Alice followed him, and everything on the stage began to change. The tree vanished, and the walls and floor became a black-and-white checkerboard. Suddenly, Pink Rabbit and Alice were falling down from the ceiling on strings. Pink Rabbit didn't look scared at all. He is used to flying through the air with me!

He reached the ground and then elegantly danced off the stage, still glancing at the pocket watch.

The show continued, and we watched as the stage was transformed again and again. There was a magical forest with a giant caterpillar, and a garden of dazzling colorful flowers who all danced across the stage with Alice. There was a tea party and a mad hatter and a glittering pink-striped cat with a huge grin. And, of course, there

was Pink Rabbit! He came dancing onto the stage often, twirling and swirling and leaping and bounding.

"That was magical!" said Zoe when the curtain came down to show it was time for the intermission.

"It was!" I agreed.

The audience started to chatter, and people all around us began standing up to go to the restroom and to get refreshments.

"Did you see that little pink rabbit?" I heard one man say behind me. "He was spectacular, wasn't he?"

"Yes," said another man. "I don't know how they made him so small. It was like magic!"

"He was an excellent dancer," said someone else. "The star of the show!"

"And so original that he was pink," said a lady nearby. "Usually the Rabbit in *Alice in Wonderland* is white!"

I felt my mouth widen into a huge smile. Pink Rabbit *had* been spectacular, and I was so proud.

Mom and Dad and all my friends began to gather around me then.

"Isadora," Dad said, "was that really Pink Rabbit on the stage?"

"What was he doing there?" asked Bruno.

"Yes, Isadora, how did it happen?" said Sashi.

I tried my best to explain everything
before the end of the intermission. I was so
busy explaining that I didn't even get to eat
the strawberry ice cream that Miss Cherry
had handed out to everyone.

"Wow!" said all my friends.

"Good for Pink Rabbit!" said Dad.

"I always knew he had talent," said Mom.

I looked around at them all and beamed.

The second half of the show was shorter. We watched as the stage was transformed into more magical wonderlands. Alice, Pink Rabbit, and the other characters danced through them, glittering and whirling in their brightly colored costumes.

At the end of the show, all the dancers came onto the stage.

They bowed together, and the audience clapped and cheered. Then Alice made a curtsy, and the audience clapped and cheered some more. I noticed one of the dancers push Pink Rabbit gently to the front of the stage. He took his own bow. Suddenly, the audience members were on their feet, stamping and whooping and cheering.

Mom waved her wand, and a bouquet
of roses exploded in the air and fell down
around Pink Rabbit.

"Fantastic!" yelled the audience. "He was magical!"

Pink Rabbit puffed out his chest, and I could tell he was extremely happy. He was pinker than ever!

Once the thick velvet curtain was lowered, the lights came back on in the theater. Everyone stood up to go home.

"We need to wait for Pink Rabbit," I said to Miss Cherry.

"Of course," she said.

We had to wait a long time before Pink Rabbit appeared from backstage with a limping Tatiana Tutu.

"I'm sorry we took so long," said Tatiana. "Everyone wanted Pink Rabbit's autograph!"

She smiled down at him. "He was terrific!" she said. "The star of the show! We are so grateful to him. And also to you, Isadora, for lending him to us!"

She held out a box. It was wrapped in shiny paper and tied with a ribbon.

"It's a present for you, to say thank you," she explained. "You and Pink Rabbit really saved the day!"

"Thank you!" I said, blushing.

"You're welcome," said Tatiana Tutu. Then she lifted her hand and waved goodbye to us all.

Chapter
Ten

The train journey home seemed very slow. Pink Rabbit was tired after his day of dancing, and he slept curled up in my lap for the whole journey. I wanted to open my present, but Mom wouldn't let me. She hid it away in her bag.

"Save it until you get home," she said.

"It might seem a little unfair to the others."

Zoe and I talked about the show and looked out the window at the darkening sky. Little flakes of snow had started to fall. They were like tiny twirling ballerinas.

"I hope I can be a ballerina one day," I said dreamily.

"Me too," said Zoe.

I gazed down at Pink Rabbit sleeping peacefully on my knee, and I stroked his ears.

"It was wonderful to see him on the stage today," I said. "I wouldn't change a thing about it. But . . . but . . . at the same time, I am a little disappointed I never got to see Tatiana Tutu dance. I would have loved to see her dancing."

"I'm sure you will someday," said Zoe reassuringly.

It was dark by the time we got to the station. We all walked back to the school together, and then my friends' parents started arriving to pick them up.

"That's the last one!" said Dad, ticking a name off his clipboard.

"Excellent," said Miss Cherry. "Thank you so much for volunteering, Mr. and Mrs. Moon."

"No problem at all," said Dad cheerfully.

"It was an experience. I have never been on a human school trip before."

"Nor have I," said Mom, taking off her safety vest and handing it back to Miss Cherry. "It was lovely to see the ballet. The dancers looked almost like fairies!"

Dad seemed reluctant to take off his safety vest.

"I didn't realize I had to give it back," he said disappointedly.

"I'm afraid so," said Miss Cherry. "It's school property."

"I thought you hated it!" said Mom in surprise.

"Well, it's grown on me," admitted Dad. "It's a very striking look, don't you think? Maybe I will ask for one for my birthday."

★ ★ ★

Mom, Dad, and I flew home through the snow, picking up Honeyblossom on the way.

"Can I open the present now?" I asked as soon as we got home.

"Of course," said Mom, handing the gift to me.

I let Pink Rabbit tear off the wrapping paper, and then we peered into the box.

"Wow!" I cried.

Tatiana Tutu's famous star diamond tiara winked up at me from a nest of pink tissue paper. I lifted it out carefully and put it on my head.

"Look!" I said to Mom and Dad. "Look!"

"Oh my goodness!" said Mom. "That is so beautiful."

"How kind of Tatiana Tutu," said Dad. "It fits you perfectly, Isadora."

Pink Rabbit continued to rustle in the box. When he came up, he was wiggling his ears in delight and holding a set of tickets in his paws.

"Family tickets to Tatiana Tutu's next ballet show!" said Mom. "You will get to see her dance after all!"

"Really?!" I said, a huge grin spreading over my face.

"Really," said Dad.

I almost felt like crying because Tatiana Tutu had been so kind.

"I didn't do very much!" I said. "All I did was knock on her door to see if she was all right, and then lend her Pink Rabbit for the show."

"Well, it was still very nice of you," said Mom. "Not everyone would have done that. It may have seemed like a small thing to you, but to Tatiana Tutu it was huge! You saved the show."

"It is always important to be kind," said Dad. "In big ways and small."

I nodded, and Pink Rabbit nodded too.

"We will always try," I said.

"Great," said Dad. "How about you be kind right now and get me some red juice from the fridge, then? It's almost breakfast time, and I'm starving!"

STAGE DOOR

Sink your fangs into
Isadora Moon's next adventure!

ISADORA MOON

Has a Birthday

Cake? Check. Games? Check.
Exploding presents? Uh-oh.

Harriet Muncaster

When the time came to start planning my birthday party, Mom and Dad seemed to be very organized.

"Leave it to us," they said. "We don't need any help."

"Are you sure you know what you're doing?" I asked nervously.

"Oh yes!" said Dad. "We've got all the ideas written down: hot potato, magician, cake, balloons, presents, bouncy castle, costumes, party favors . . ."

"It's going to be the best birthday party ever!" said Mom.

"We need to have invitations," I told them. "Don't forget the invitations."

Dad frowned and scratched his head. Then he wrote "invitations" at the bottom of the list.

The next day at school, we were in a math lesson when suddenly there came a great flapping sound from outside.

"What on earth is that?" said Miss Cherry, darting toward the window.

A swarm of envelopes were flying through the air on little bat wings, and now they were tapping against the windows, trying to get in.

"Oh my goodness!" Miss Cherry exclaimed.

I felt my face go red with embarrassment.

"Let them in!" cried Oliver. "Let's see what they are!"

"Don't let them in!" wailed shy Samantha, ducking down behind her desk.

The envelopes kept beating their wings against the glass until one of them found an open window. It beckoned to the others. Then they all came flying in, fluttering and flapping, landing one by one on my friends' desks.

"It's an invitation!" cried Oliver once he had ripped his envelope open.

"A birthday party!" yelled Zoe. "At Isadora's house!"

"It's a costume party!" shouted someone else. "I love costumes!"

All the children were chatting excitedly, but Miss Cherry did not look too pleased. Now that she had got over her surprise, she seemed just a tiny bit annoyed.

"Isadora," she said, "it's not really appropriate to make such a scene in the middle of a lesson."

I slunk down in my chair and felt like I wanted to disappear.

"Sorry," I whispered.

DEAR: Oliver

You're invited to Isadora Moon's Birthday Party!

WHEN: This Saturday

WHERE: The big pink-and-black house

TIME: 10 AM – 3 PM

RSVP

P.S. Please wear a costume!

Harriet Muncaster

Harriet Muncaster, that's me! I'm the author and illustrator of Isadora Moon.

Yes, really! I love anything teeny-tiny, anything starry, and everything glittery.

New friends. New adventures.
Find a new series . . . just for you!

FOR THE SPORTS FAN

FOR THE ADVENTURER

FOR THE SUPERSTAR

FOR THE DREAMER

FOR THE ANIMAL LOVER

FOR THE EXPLORER

RandomHouseKids.com